SINGLE DAD'S CHRISTMAS GIFT

IRIS WEST

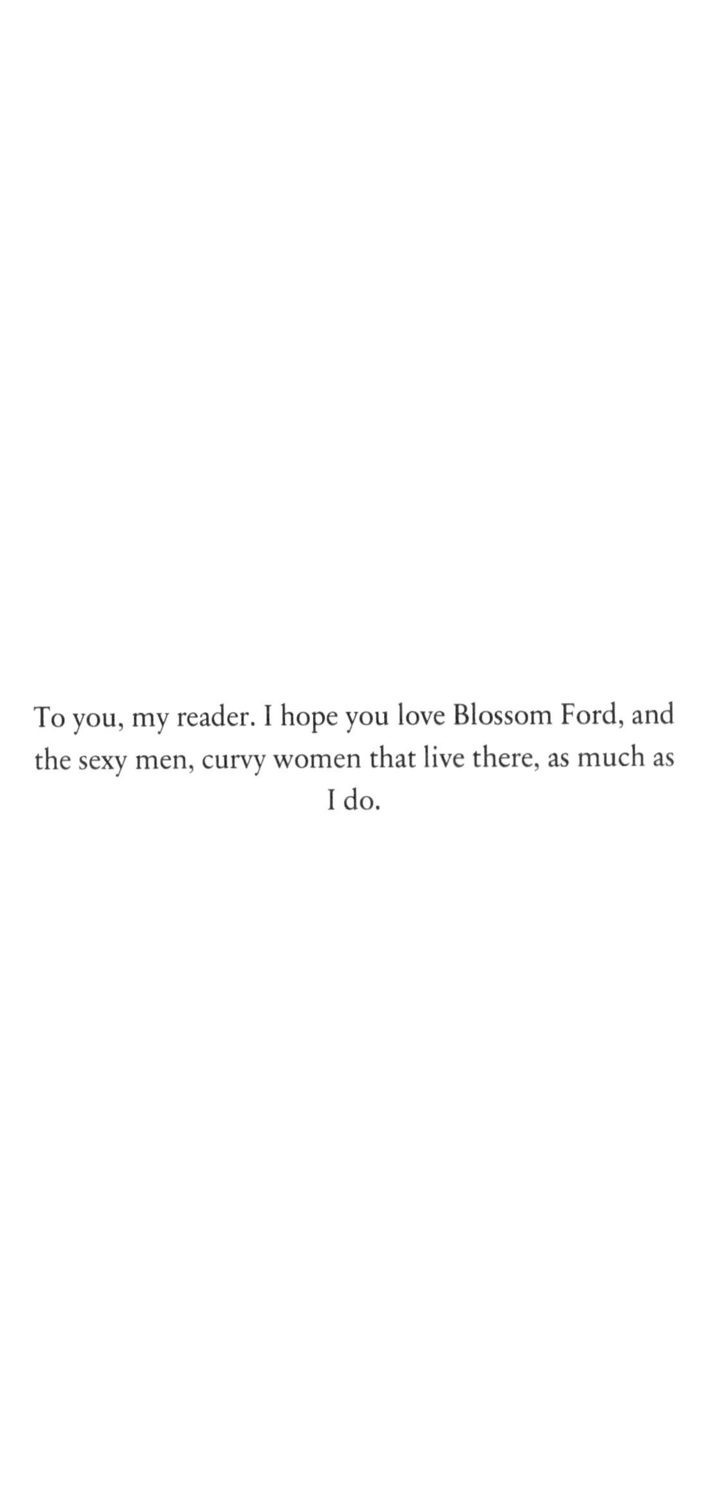

To you, my reader. I hope you love Blossom Ford, and the sexy men, curvy women that live there, as much as I do.

CHAPTER ONE

Layla

I SHOULD BE embarrassed to feel the excitement bubbling through me. Yes, it's Friday afternoon and I'm about to finish work for the week. However, I know what Friday afternoon anticipation feels like and this is not it. My heart is beating a little too fast, my eyes keep darting beyond the classroom door, the playground and the fencing surrounding the school; seeking the tall figure of a man, they have no right to linger on.

Never, in my one and a half years of teaching, have I been this excited at the prospect of seeing a parent.

Neither have you ever come across a dad like Fallon O'Connor.

The thought slips into my mind and I latch onto it, desperately trying to assuage the guilt that runs through me every time I think about Fallon, especially in front of my innocent third graders.

I'm a healthy young woman. It's perfectly normal to be fantasizing about the most gorgeous man in town. The other female teachers do it too, even the married ones. I can tell by the way they look at him. I don't know if they go as far as thinking about him in the privacy of their beds or showers, like I do. The point is, they can't help themselves either. The man is too damn gorgeous for a human male.

I remind myself that the object of my desire is not Fallon to me, despite the number of times I call him that when my hands are roving down his back in my fantasies. He's Mr. O'Connor.

Slowly, I get out of my chair and drop myself in front of my students, crossing my legs like theirs. I can't see outside the school fence when I'm sitting on the carpet.

"Miss. Shah, what story are you going to tell us?" Evie asks, gray eyes wide.

And just like that, my mind is suddenly clear. My students deserve the best of me. Also, I'm the type of teacher who always puts her kid's interests first, like Mom.

I shove aside a pang of guilt, especially towards Evie, as it's her hunk of a father I've been lusting over.

Several stories flash across my mind, and I sift through them until I settle on one. I clap twice to get the kids' attention and when they clap back, then fall silent, I begin. Using my hands and body, I act the story, the delight on the faces of my audience a balm to my soul. I'm so engrossed in the story I'm startled when the bell rings just as I'm acting the last few words.

I let the children out until only Evie is in the classroom with me.

"Something must have delayed your dad, sweetheart. He's usually the first one here."

Evie looks at the playground then shrugs, but her eyes are full of worry. She slips a tiny hand into mine.

I crouch and pat her head with my free hand, smoothing the soft braid on her head.

"I'm sure he'll be here soon. Wanna bet?"

Interest replaces the worry in those eyes that remind me so much of her father.

"If we spy your dad in the next two minutes, I win. If he's not here by then, you win."

"What do I get if I win?"

"Well," I look back into the classroom. "You can color one page in my special drawing book."

Evie's lips make an o.

"If I win, you have to do some jobs for me in the classroom during recess, on Monday."

"Okay."

I grab a stopwatch from my desk, and we set the timer together.

My lips lift. Evie's eyes lock on the watch.

"There's your dad, I say, about a minute later."

My voice is low. I clear my throat but can't pull my

eyes away from Fallon O'Connor's long and sturdy, jean-clad legs. His red plaid button-down shirt and dark green coat make an attractive contrast to his short beard and brown windswept hair.

Stormy gray eyes stare back and I remember I'm his daughter's teacher.

"You won, Miss. Shah."

Evie shakes my hand from side to side, and her enthusiasm makes me smile.

"What did Miss. Shah win?" Evie's dad asks, eyes as curious as his daughter's.

"A game we were playing," Evie answers and waves goodbye to me.

Her father watches her stalk out of the classroom until she stops in the middle of the playground. I watch the little girl too, my heart going out to her as well as her dad, just like it did the first day of school, three and a half months ago.

All the other kids were playing while their parents chatted in small groups. Fallon and Evie were the only odd ones out, both standing awkwardly, the small distance between their stiff bodies a statement that something wasn't right between them. There were rumors around town saying Fallon O'Connor was childless until last Christmas but turned up in town with a seven-year-old during summer break. And it looked like he was back for good.

"Here's Evie's costume," he says in his deep, lilting voice.

I take Evie's nativity play costume from him and nod, unable to trust my voice.

"A button fell off. I was sewing it, that's why I'm late."

"Evie has enjoyed helping you make it. She talked about it the whole week."

He looks back at Evie, and I just know he's checking on her.

Warmth fills my heart and I confirm what I've been suspecting for a while now. It isn't only lust I feel for Mr. Wrong, I'm fast developing a crush for him. I'm helpless in the face of the way he cares for his daughter. He could have bought the nativity costume or asked his mom to make it, but he'd made the king's cape and crown with Evie.

He'd asked questions about what to make, as if he were discussing something that affected lives. I almost told him not to take it seriously, but his expression stopped me. It was a serious issue for him. He wanted Evie to love the costume he made. Watching him desperately try to win his daughter's heart is making me fall for him.

I inhale deeply, trying to regulate my thumping heart.

"She talks about you to Mom all the time, too. She loves coming to school."

His stormy grey eyes are direct. A smile hovers around his lips, making me want to see his lips lift until he's smiling fully. I can't help feeling he'd look great smiling fully.

An expression I don't understand comes over his face. I blink. By the time I'm gazing at him again, whatever it is has disappeared.

"Have a good weekend, Ms. Shah."

I watch him walk towards Evie, his broad back straight. He extends his hand. I hold my breath. After what seems like a long time, Evie places her hand in his. I exhale, relief flooding through me. A silly smile spreads over my face, but I don't care.

Fallon O'Connor has been trying to hold his daughter's hand since the first day of school. Every time, Evie ignored him. Today is the first time she's held it.

I tell myself the reason I'm giddy with happiness is my student. When she first came to school, Evie wouldn't talk or play with other kids. It's taken a lot of coaxing to make her feel safe enough to open up. She's made a couple of friends and is more talkative in class. So, it's perfectly natural for me to be ecstatic at seeing her relationship with her dad improve.

When they pass the gate, I close the door of my classroom, head to my chair and collapse onto it. Because I just thought about Fallon O'Connor. Unconsciously, I imagined the pleasure and relief he must have felt when his daughter held his hand.

I sit and shake my head, forcing myself to face reality. Fallon O'Connor is off limits to me. We're not meant for each other. First, he's my student's dad. Sure, technically there's no law against a teacher dating a parent and John Gibbons Elementary doesn't forbid it, but it's frowned upon. I've been in town for just over sixteen months and finally feel like I'm settling down. I don't want rumors to spread about me. And I love my job too much to create any tension in school.

Second, would Fallon O'Connor ever be interested in me? Where Evie is concerned, he always seems to be at a loss. However, I know he's a capable person because of the questions he asks when he wants my help with Evie's homework or there's an issue with her behavior. In every other aspect, he's way ahead of me. Older, more experienced, one of the best E. R doctors in the country. Now that he's back in town, there's a line of more experienced women vying for his attention. It's a hot topic of conversation amongst the female teachers at school.

Even if by a miracle he fancies me, am I ready for a relationship? Can I trust another man after what happened with Dean? Drooling over Fallon O'Connor must mean I'm over my ex-fiancée's betrayal, but that doesn't mean I'm ready to trust another man.

I stand and tidy up the classroom. I'm going to do what I've been doing since Fallon O'Connor rolled into town with his smoking eyes and hot body. Spend more time with my BOB, my trusty battery-operated boyfriend. BOB is safe and gives me uncomplicated pleasure.

My life is fulfilling. I love teaching kids. The

knitting club, movies and prosecco make my evenings and weekends enjoyable. It's enough.

CHAPTER TWO

Fallon

I'M SO CHOKED up that for the first time since I met Evie ten months ago, I don't mind her silence. Her hand is tiny against mine, but she's holding on tight. I stare at our joined hands and swallow. Since taking my hand, Evie hasn't looked at me.

I help her into the truck, walk around to the driver's side and climb in.

"What did you do today?" I ask the back of her head once I pull away.

She's gazing at the Christmas trees, lights and inflatable Santas along St. Lucia Street.

"Played."

"Who did you play with?" I try to remember all the

children I heard her mention to my parents, Auntie Caitlin, or one of my brothers.

"My friend."

"Tommy? The boy with the horn-rimmed glasses?"

I stop at a traffic light and gaze at her in time to catch the shake of her head.

"Ricky?" Once, Evie told Mom the boy was upset because a few of the children in the class teased him for having ginger hair.

"No."

I think for a moment, then recall Ms. Shah mentioning that sometimes Evie played with another girl in the school.

"Suzie?"

"Yes."

"What did you play?"

"Games."

"Were they fun?"

Evie draws shapes on the window. It's her signal she won't answer any more questions.

I stop myself from sighing. Evie's talked for longer than usual. On top of holding my hand, it's a tremendous improvement in our relationship. I shouldn't be greedy and want more, but I can't help it.

At first, when I brought Evie home, she didn't talk to anyone. She watched everyone with fear in her huge eyes. After a few weeks, she opened up to my parents and Auntie Caitlin. She willingly sat with them and held their hands. One day, she talked. She said little, but I was overjoyed she started trusting someone, even if it wasn't me. However, as weeks passed, and she opened up with my brothers, then later with Layla and the children in her class, it became increasingly hard not to feel jealous.

I understand the science behind her behavior towards me. Her therapist explained it. Evie lived with only her mom her whole life. When her mom died, she lost everything meaningful to her. Her mom introduced us a few months before she passed, but the scared six-year-old child that she was then probably couldn't understand why he hadn't been a dad to her before.

I can't say I blame Evie. Finding out I had a six-year-old was shocking. Evie's mom and I were sexual partners for six months before she left New York. I used a condom, and she was on the pill. The chances of her conceiving were almost non-existent.

In February, she called and said I was a father. She'd taken medication, which interfered with the pill, so she thought taking care of Evie was her responsibility. She was ill and wanted to give me the option of taking care of the child before securing the services of a caregiver or boarding school.

I gaze at Evie, who's still staring out the window. If it was hard for me to understand, how could a young child do so? One day, she'll feel safe enough to trust that I love her and am in her life to stay. However long it takes, I must be patient.

Today, I made progress. I'm going to enjoy that. I have one more week of taking Evie to school. After winter break, I start work at Weston-Parker General. I'm going to miss doing the school run.

And not just because of Evie.

An image of Layla's curvy body flashes across my mind. The way her full, round hips - almost double the width of her shoulders - hugged the soft gray woolen material of the skirt she was wearing is imprinted in my mind. Along with the enticing way, her turtleneck sweater clung to breasts and slim waist. My hand tightens on the wheel.

Where it concerns Evie's teacher, my mind seems to notice every detail, even when I'm worried about stuff.

I inhale. Deeply.

My dick is not the only part of me that's obsessed with the young woman. My mind keeps replaying how the golden flakes in her green eyes shine when she smiles. It imagines how warm and safe my daughter must have felt a few weeks ago when the teacher hugged her - Evie looked dreamy when she told mom about it.

It gobbles up everything my little girl says about her. I know what a wonderful storyteller she is. How she punishes the kids if they are being mean to other kids. The rewards she hands out for good behavior.

Mom and Auntie Caitlin sing her praises too. She's in their knitting club and works so hard at making scarves and mittens to donate to orphanages and homeless shelters.

However, I have no right to be thinking about the innocent woman. She's starting out her life while I have a kid to bring up. I'm married to my work, always have been. Every woman I've been with has knowingly been a mistress. They've always come second to my career. That's why I only get involved with career women who want the same thing.

I can't imagine the sweet teacher ever agreeing to a relationship like that. And for some perverse reason, I'm glad. She deserves a charming young man who's willing to marry her and give her a houseful of babies.

My knuckles turn white. I force myself to bite back a string of swear words. I'm trying my hardest to keep a clean mouth around Evie, but the thought of Layla with another man drives me insane.

I force myself to relax the fingers on the steering wheel. As I turn off the road and enter a gate with the sign O'Connor Premium Farms above it, I remind myself that I'm struggling with Evie and need no more complications.

CHAPTER THREE

Layla

I'M AT THE movie theatre trying to decide whether to have sweet or salty popcorn. The teenager on the till taps his fingers on the counter.

"Would you like a taste of each?" His voice is dripping with honey.

"I'll have it sweet, please."

Despite it being Friday evening, the place is almost empty. I suppose most people are doing their Christmas shopping. I grab my drink and popcorn and head to the auditorium. There's no one there.

I choose a middle seat in the back row and make myself comfortable. It's the last viewing of the movie. I might be the only person watching it. That's never happened before. I thought I'd love it. Now, it feels kind of lonely.

I remember Evie hasn't watched the movie. All the other kids in the class watched it with their families. She would love it. Thinking about Evie brings Fallon O'Connor to my mind.

I left home to stop thinking about him, so I remind myself what the movie is about, trying to drive him out of my head.

The sound of a door opening has me perking my ears. Maybe I'll have company. To avoid being caught staring, I grab my drink and take a long sip of cold soda. When I glance up, my eyes collide with Fallon's.

He and Evie are standing a few steps down from my row. I blink. He says something to Evie, points to seats on the opposite side of where I'm sitting.

Evie shakes her head, then glances around. I can tell the moment she spots me. Her pixie face creases into a huge smile, and she waves. I'm unable to resist her infectious smile.

She heads my way. Fallon stops her. I gaze at my popcorn, pretending not to notice how the wet lock of hair that fell to one side of his face makes him look more approachable.

Even from my seat, I can tell he's had a shower. He replaced the red button down with a blue dress shirt and the blue jeans with black ones. He's looking more handsome than he was this afternoon.

I bite my lip. Will I be able to concentrate on the movie?

Suddenly, they're walking towards me. I stand,

reminding myself of my role. They must be coming up to say hello. Blossom Ford is a small town. I've had parents stop me for a chat in many places.

I respond to Evie's greeting and am glad of the way my voice is professional when I greet her father.

"May we please sit with you, Miss?" Evie asks.

There's so much hope and faith in the little girl's eyes that I want to say yes. I can no longer deny I have a soft spot for this child. And the feeling goes beyond the affection one feels for a favorite pupil.

"Please don't feel pressured into accepting. I've explained that this is your free time. You don't have to sit with us. We understand that, don't we, poppet?"

Evie nods, but her eyes plead with me. My heart goes all mushy and the professional in me disappears, leaving behind the woman who's in love with this little girl who has suffered so much.

I glance around. Apart from us, there's no one else. Surely the movie is about to start. Nobody will know about this.

"It's okay, if you don't mind, Mr. O'Connor."

He stares at me, his gray eyes unreadable. Then he looks at Evie. His eyes soften, and that changes his whole face. My heart goes all mushy again. The love he feels for his little girl shines brightly in his usually unreadable face.

"Okay," he agrees.

Evie wraps her arms around her father's thighs and thanks him.

Fallon stares at his daughter as if fascinated.

Just as suddenly as she initiated the contact, Evie's arms fall away, and she darts into the seat beside me. Her dad follows slowly, still dazed by her display of affection.

I sit and ask Evie a question about the movie. While she's replying, the lights go out. I marvel at how much she talks now compared to when she first came to school.

Under the cover of darkness, I watch as Fallon places a bucket of popcorn on Evie's lap and shows her the drink in the cup holder. He's gentle, more open when he interacts with her.

It's the opposite of how he's with me. He's always guarded. Almost unapproachable. As if he feels the scrutiny, he turns towards me. I don't know how much he can see, but heat flushes my face.

"It's starting," Evie says.

Relieved, I turn towards the screen.

When I still can't focus on the trailers on the screen, I grab my drink. Maybe the delicious rush of sugar will help. A few minutes after the movie begins, I'm lost in the story. Halfway through, I'm so horrified by what's happening to the main character that I jump when Evie clutches my arm. That's when I realize she's just as engrossed as I am.

"Here," Fallon whispers.

He's holding out a tissue. I grab it, thank him, and wonder if I spilled my drink when I feel the wetness on my checks. And I'm embarrassed all over again.

A thumping sound grabs my attention and I'm caught up in the film again. It's not until the credits roll and the lights switch on that I become aware Fallon is staring at Evie and me.

I avoid his gaze.

"What did you think?" I ask Evie.

"Epic!"

I chuckle.

"It was epic," I agree with her.

I put my coat on, grab my empty popcorn backet and cup.

Fallon stands with his and Evie's empty containers in one hand and holds up his other hand for Evie. In the foyer, we bin the containers, then leave the quiet theater.

There are a lot more cars in the small parking lot than when I arrived. Their owners must be here to watch the other movie, which has just started showing. It's a relief. Whilst we are not technically doing anything wrong, I don't want any rumors to spread.

It's windier and colder than when I headed out earlier in the evening.

"We'll give you a lift."

"I'll be fine walking. I don't live far."

"It's on our way. It'd be silly for us to leave you to walk when it's this dark and cold."

Evie slips her hand into mine and takes a step forward. Making me remember her first day at school.

She'd refused to go into the classroom. I gave her a bright smile, slipped my hand in her small one and stepped forward too. She'd been so startled that she'd followed me.

We must look like a family of three, but I don't have the heart to pull my hand out of the little girl's.

I sit in the back with Evie. She's so excited about the movie that we talk non-stop.

"It's the best movie ever!" Evie says.

"It was great, but The Chronicle Of Narnia is the best movie ever."

"I haven't watched that. It must be double epic then," she says.

"What do you think, Mr. O'Connor? Was the movie your favorite?" I can't help asking when I catch him gazing at us in the rear-view mirror.

"It was EPIC, but I doubt there'll ever be a better movie than Toy Story."

He pulls up outside my house.

I smile at the way he said the word epic.

Evie hugs me. I embrace her and caress her hair.

"Goodnight Evie."

"Night Miss. Shah. See you Monday."

Fallon opens the door of the truck, and I climb out.

"Thank you so much for the ride."

"You made Evie's evening. She loved your company."

The light of the moon and streetlamp casts shadows on his face. However, I can tell by the sound of his voice that he's not as guarded as he's been before. He sounds friendlier.

How the heck am I supposed to resist this version of Fallon O'Connor?

CHAPTER FOUR

Fallon

I'M OUTSIDE LAYLA'S apartment building the next morning, on an errand for Mom to deliver a large donation of knitted goods to one of the nearby towns. Spending more time with the sweet teacher is a terrible idea, but I couldn't get out of it. I'm standing in for Mr. Potts, a member of Mom's knitting club, who had an accident and can't make the trip.

Layla comes out of the building with a picnic bag slung over her shoulder. She's wearing jeans and sneakers and a red knitted beanie. Her long braid peaks out of the beanie and hangs over her shoulder. A knitted scarf the same color as the beanie wraps around her neck.

She climbs in and I close the door behind her.

"I hope this trip is not a huge inconvenience for

you," she says when I ease onto the road.

I can't really tell her I'm worried I'll give in to the urge to stop the car and kiss her lush, pink lips.

"I have the time. Mom's taking Evie to the mall, so this is nothing. Shall we call each other by our first names? It's a three hour round trip. It'll be silly to be formal."

"Sure."

She turns to the boxes at the back of the truck.

"You should have picked me up so I could help load the truck."

"I needed the exercise."

What I really needed was to spend as little time as possible in her company. I spent a lot of time in the movie theatre studying her instead of watching the screen. In the semi-darkness of the auditorium, it was hard to see clearly however, her reactions fascinated me.

Watching Evie and Layla laugh together and exclaim over the movie made me wonder what it would be like to be a real family. It was the first time I ever thought that.

I've never been tempted to marry before. I was so busy being an E. R. doctor and teaching in New York City that I never wanted a wife to feel lonely.

Before Evie, I lived with a woman who was also a doctor. Like me, her work was the most important thing in her life and she just wanted the occasional sexual and dining companion. She couldn't handle me having Evie. It disrupted our usual pattern. She moved out a week after I took Evie to New York.

Even when I resigned from my job in New York City and moved to Blossom Ford, where I'd be working fewer hours, marriage wasn't part of my plan. Evie had plenty of female family role models in Mom and Auntie Caitlin. I have eight brothers, so she was already part of a large family.

Layla changed that. And now, I can't stop wondering. So, yes, time away from Layla would help me sort out my thoughts.

It snows before we leave town. A few flakes are stuck to the humongous Christmas tree on the town square.

Layla is looking too. A smile hovers around her lips. She's so transparent. Like Evie, I can tell what she's thinking.

"I have blankets in the back. Tell me if you feel cold."

"It's warm in here."

She unwraps her scarf and lets it hang loose around her neck.

"I brought coffee if you fancy it. It's not a long trip and there are a couple of rest stops along the way, but Mr. Potts likes carrot cake, so I made some."

"I'll have to try it then. Auntie Caitlin says your carrot cake is better than Mom's. I won't believe that until I try some."

"Now that's a compliment. I love your mom's cooking and baking. If my mom wasn't such a superb cook, I'd be jealous of you."

"Exactly! I'll try it when we've handed over the boxes."

"So, Toy Story?"

I frown at her.

"Is that a condescending note I hear?"

"Of course not. It's just so stereotypical."

"Why do I feel you're laughing at me?"

She chuckles.

"Sorry, I didn't mean to laugh."

"You did."

I'm pretending I'm offended, but I'm not. I love seeing her laugh like this.

"It's an action movie. From what I've seen, most guys like love action films. I just thought you'd say something different."

"What made you think that?"

"The way you care about Evie. You're not like most dads I've met. They care about their children, but most are not so hands on. Or understanding psychological issues like the one Evie is going through. Maybe it's because you're a doctor."

"Are you saying that for a man, I'm not macho enough, Miss. Shah?" I growl.

"No!"

I laugh, unable to keep a straight face at the way she's flustered. I stop at a red light and watch her.

She stares at me. Her eyes narrow, then she's laughing too.

"Maybe I deserved that."

"I didn't mean to laugh," I repeat her words.

She laughs harder.

"I'll remember to never cross you," she says.

"Toy Story wasn't just an action movie, though. Did you watch it?"

"It's actually my dad's favorite. So, I've watched it like, a hundred times."

"Your dad has good taste. The movie is colorful, hilarious and heartfelt. It's about friendship and growing up. It's one of those movies that anyone, whatever their age, can relate to."

"That's exactly what he says. We're a big movie family. So, we take turns deciding what to watch. Dad always wants to watch Toy Story."

"You sound like you miss your family."

"Not as much as last year. This is my second academic year in Blossom Ford; I'm getting used to being away from home."

"Garnet City is only a few hours away. You can easily visit it on weekends."

"That's right. The snow is becoming heavier, isn't it?"

Why do I have the feeling she's changing the subject? I wonder what made a young woman like Layla, who seems to love her family, move to Blossom Ford? She clearly loves her job, but could have easily found a teaching post in her hometown.

Everyone in town seems to think something made

her leave Garnet City, but no one knows what. Whilst her face is an open book, she's clearly good at keeping secrets.

"It's windier too. It'll probably clear up soon. There was nothing on the forecast about the bad weather. But the trees look amazing."

I gaze at the towering pine trees on the sides of the highway. They'd make a pretty picture for a postcard.

"I think more snow is on the way," I say after studying the sky.

CHAPTER FIVE

Layla

I CAN'T BELIEVE I fell asleep. The first thing I realize when I come to is the car is stationary. Then, a delicious scent of spicy musk hits my nostrils. I open my eyes and freeze. Fallon is inches away from me. I only have to lift my head a little and we'll be kissing.

His eyes are stormier than I've ever seen them and they're fixed on my lips. He wants to kiss me. My heart thumps so loudly, it's all I can hear. He stares at me, a question in his eyes.

I move closer, giving him permission, hungry for his touch.

A loud noise distracts me. Fallon glances at the window of the truck. Someone is knocking on the car window. Fallon returns to his seat and rolls the window down.

"Are you dropping off the knitted goods for the orphanage and homeless shelter?" An elderly man asks after greeting us. "I'll show you where they are going and help you unpack," he says when we nod.

It's so cold outside that I reach back in for the scarf and beanie I took off earlier.

"A storm is coming. You want to get out of here as soon as possible, or you'll get caught in it. It's just as well you have the right car to drive in this weather."

He guides us through the door of a community center and leads us to a small room in the back of the building. Another man is there, moving boxes to one side of the room.

It only takes a few minutes for the four of us to unload the truck.

"Thank you for bringing these. They'll make nice holiday gifts. A lot of folks will be mighty glad to get them," the elderly gentleman says. He hands Fallon two large cake tins. "Give this to your mom; she's expecting it. My wife made it. She used to knit all the time, but now her fingers can't cope with it. It's for everyone in the knitting club. We could give you a cup of tea, but I think you'd be better off leaving right away if you want to get home today."

"His wife started the knitting club. She's from Blossom Ford, moved here when she married," I say after we drive away.

While unloading the truck, I forgot what happened earlier. Now I'm enclosed in the truck with Fallon; it's all I can think about. I'm sure Fallon was going to kiss me. And I wanted him to. Badly.

In that moment, all I could think about was touching him, feeling his skin against mine. I've fantasized about him touching me, but that's all it was. Never did I believe I'd have a chance to actually kiss him. Now it almost happened; I think I'll go insane thinking about it.

When did he become attracted to me? He's shown no signs. Was it a spur-of-the-moment thing? Maybe something made him horny, and I was there. Should I pretend it didn't happen?

I glance at Fallon. What's he thinking? He's leaning forward, assessing the sky.

I look ahead and really take in the conditions of the road. While I was worrying over the moment between us, the snow started falling faster. The wipers are going at full speed, but it's becoming harder to see.

"Are we going to make it?"

"We'll be fine if the weather doesn't deteriorate."

The worse happens. Fallon slows down as visibility worsens drastically. I've never seen anything like it. It's like a freak storm.

About twenty minutes later, we're crawling.

"We're going to have to stop. It doesn't look like this storm is going to stop soon. It's dangerous to go on without knowing what might happen."

Alarm spreads through me.

"Here?"

Snow covered pine trees stretch towards the skies on our sides. The crying of the wind is so loud, it's eerie. It would be great to record it as an audio prompt to improve my kids' writing, but the prospect of having to stop here just reminded me of the horrifying fact that people can freeze to death in their cars.

If the wind gets any stronger, there's also the possibility of a branch, maybe a tree falling on us.

"There's an old hunting cabin nearby," Fallon says.

"Can you reach it?" I see nothing. Will he be able to find his way there?

"A few times. I used to follow my brother Verlin and his best friend when they came to explore the forest here."

The image of a young Fallon persistently bothering his older brother and friend makes me smile and, for a moment, I forget how dangerous our situation is.

On the left, a narrow clearing of trees becomes visible. Fallon eases the truck onto the space and inches forward.

"It isn't a fancy place, but we should be able to start a fire."

The sound of something heavy cracking startles me. A bang follows it. I turn towards Fallon, and can just make out a dark shape on the ground, inches from the crawling truck.

"What's that?"

"Can you take out the torch in the glove compartment?"

"What?"

"Grab the torch in the glove compartment."

I obey him.

"Good. Now check it works."

I click the on button. A powerful beam of light flashes.

"A pack of batteries was beside it. Grab that as well."

The truck stops.

"We're here," Fallon says.

I sigh in relief that we've arrived, and the truck didn't stop because we broke down.

Fallon switches off the engine and climbs out. "Wait a minute."

I get out as well.

He glares at me.

"I'll stay by the door." I'm not letting him out of my sight. The only thing I can think of right now is calling for help. My phone has no reception; I checked earlier. I'm positive no one could come out in this weather, anyway. Fallon has the skills to survive in this situation, I don't. Seeing him makes me feel safe.

The cabin is made of wood and doesn't look like it's big.

Fallon bends and moves a stone aside. He picks up something which I figure out is a key the moment he inserts it into the lock on the door. He shines the torch around the inside for about a minute.

"Get your bag. Be careful on the snow."

He strides to the back of the truck and carries out a

loaded crate.

"What's that?" I ask, clutching my bag.

"Emergency supplies."

I follow him into the wooden cabin.

CHAPTER SIX

Layla

IT'S THREE IN the afternoon yet it's so dark outside, it feels like nighttime. I'm glad I used the toilet before we left the community center; there isn't one here. I wouldn't feel comfortable taking care of business outside on my own. Asking Fallon to stand watch is out of the option.

The cabin is old, but clean. There's a small table and four unmatched chairs around it, even a few pieces of crockery. It took Fallon only a few minutes to get the fire going in the old fireplace, with logs that were neatly stacked in a corner of the room.

We ate tuna and crackers from Fallon's emergency crate; the carrot cake I made and downed it all with coffee.

I'm sitting in front of the fire, feeling warm with my

legs inside a thick sleeping bag. Even with a blanket around my shoulders, it became too cold to sit at the table. The cabin was empty too long, so with the amount of snow that fell earlier, it would take a while longer before it became warmer.

I'm feeling guilty that I'm the only one warm when the sleeping bag belongs to Fallon. He wears a coat and shirt only, which means he doesn't feel the cold so much, nevertheless, it's freezing.

"Your carrot cake is slightly better. Don't tell Mom that."

I can't stop feeling he's trying to cheer me up.

"I won't. Aren't you cold? Your sleeping bag is huge. We can share it."

Fallon gazes at my lips and I remember that almost kiss. He's a little too far; I can't read the expression in his eyes in the candlelight. Yet, there's a stillness about him that makes me wonder if he's thinking the same thing.

"Layla."

My hand tightens on the blanket. It's the first time he's ever called me by my given name. In his lilting, deep voice, it sounds like an invitation to pleasure.

"If I share that sleeping bag with you, I'm going to fuck you."

My core clenches. My nipples swell. I've never been aroused so quickly and intensely. My body is ready for Fallon.

I bite my bottom lip. He keeps staring. I try to

remember why this might be a bad idea. I don't sleep with men I haven't dated for at least two months. Didn't I do that with Dean? Look how it turned out. Being a good girl broke my heart.

Just this once. I want to touch him so badly.

"Okay." Is that throaty voice mine?

With two strides, Fallon reaches me.

He casts his blanket aside as he kneels in front of me. He reaches for the back of my neck and draws me close to him.

"I've imagined what you tasted like every night," he whispers against my lips.

Then he's kissing me like a man starved, our tongues tangling against each other. His hand slides down my back to my ass.

"I want to feel your skin against mine," he says.

Still kissing me, he helps remove my blanket. With shaky fingers, I open the zip of my coat.

He tears away from me and throws the two blankets on top of the sleeping bag. Then he's taking off his coat and boots.

"Get inside the blanket. It'll be warmer."

A laugh breaks out of me. "I'm already hot."

He watches me, a strange expression in his eyes. Then he laughs.

"You're beautiful, Layla."

My laughter stops. At that moment, I realize I'm in love with Fallon.

When he lifts his sweater, I undress as well, fighting

a sudden bout of shyness.

I scoot inside the sleeping blanket. Fallon gets in and covers us.

"What's the matter?"

He picks up my braid, unravels it, spreads the strands around my head.

"It's our first time together. Guess I'm feeling a little shy."

He pets the tip of my nose. Envelops my breasts in his hands, squeezes then pinches the pebbled tips and takes turns sucking them.

I moan. Molten heat stains my inner thighs.

Fallon slips a hand down my abdomen and strokes my folds.

"Still shy?" He rasps against my mouth.

"Hmm?"

I rub against his hand, moaning again.

"Still shy?"

"Nooo."

He slides down my body and licks his way into my core.

"You taste better than in my dreams. Your scent is driving me crazy, baby."

I hold the back of his neck to me, uncaring about how I'm losing it. I'm so close to coming.

"Fallon, more please," I gasp.

He squeezes my swollen nether lips and fingers my protruding clit, still fucking me with his tongue.

I come apart, the contractions in my core so

powerful, my back arches off the floor as I scream his name. Like a rag doll, I flop onto the sleeping bag, spent.

Fallon licks the insides of my thighs, and I realize he's swallowing my juices. Tears sting my eyes. No one has ever done that before. He's such a giving person, it's no wonder I fell in love with him.

He kisses his way up my body.

"I thought fucking you with my tongue was going to be enough. But it's not. I want inside of you, badly."

His eyes are dark, urgent.

I grab his wet hard cock, guide it to my entrance.

"I don't have a condom," he groans.

"I'm clean."

"Me too. Are you on the pill?"

"No, but it's my safe time of the month."

Fallon bites the side of my neck and penetrates me until he's buried deep in my core.

He tucks his hands under my ass and fucks me, setting a fast pace.

My pussy greedily sucks him with every thrust. It feels so good to be stretched to the fullest that I'm panting again, ready for another release. I close my eyes, savoring every moment.

"Layla! Look at me."

I open my eyes.

"You're mine now."

I feel so good, my eyelids droop.

He freezes the bulbous head of his engorged, long

shaft, a breath away from my entrance.

"Don't stop." I arch my hips.

"Say it Layla," he growls, shifting further away.

"What?" I'm staring at him now.

"Say you're mine. I want you to see who's making you scream."

"I'm yours, Fallon." I mean every word.

Wildly, he slams into me, again and again, each time somehow deeper than before.

I rake my nails down his muscled back, the frenzied storm building inside of me coming to a peak.

He sucks the bite on my neck and I contract against him, his name a song on my lips. Fallon stills, then bucks into me, shooting hot seed up my core.

CHAPTER SEVEN

Fallon

I TRY TO make as little noise as possible as I let myself into the cabin. I place some logs I collected from the outside shed in the fireplace, then put the rest in the corner. With a rag, I pick up the small kettle beside the fireplace and pour a little water into a bowl to wash my hands.

I undress and get in beside Layla. She's lying on her side, warm and soft. I rub my hands to warm them so she won't be cold when I spoon her.

The moment I touch her hip, she turns

toward me and snuggles against my chest. I smile. No woman has ever made me feel as content as I am now. I've always loved sex, but I never imagined the encompassing level of satisfaction I felt with her. I want to talk and lie like this with her every day, not just fuck her. This is the first time I've wanted more than sex with a woman. I felt that the moment I entered her.

Will she feel the same way? A pang of uncertainty gnaws at me. What about Evie? I can't hurt her. She has to be my priority. Have I finally found the love of my life only to cannot claim her?

"You don't have to worry about me. We're two consenting adults who slept together. Once we leave, I'll pretend it never happened."

I was so deep in thought I didn't realize Layla had woken up. Her words leave me cold.

"Is that how you really feel?"

She blinks at me, a frown marring the warm caramel of her skin.

"You said you're mine. Did you do that because I forced you? Or was it the heat of the moment?" I didn't know how I could be this possessive. All the sophistication I accumulated with my twenty-plus years of experience with women has vanished in an instant. I want to make her come over and over and shower her with affection until she feels there's no one who can make her as happy as I can.

Instead, I force myself to relax. She has every right to be confused. I hid my attraction to her. I'm older than her and already have a daughter. Just because she finds me attractive doesn't mean she'll want to settle with me. She may prefer someone younger, her own age.

"Isn't this casual sex for you?"

I sigh.

I'll have to be honest and take my chances with Layla.

"I meant every word I said. I don't lie, not even in the heat of the moment."

She seats up, wraps one blanket around her.

I do the same and face her.

"Does that mean you want to do this again?"

"No!"

She winces.

I rub the back of my neck.

"Layla, I fell in lust with you the day we first met."

Her eyes widen.

"Evie and I were at the back of the playground. There were so many people around you, all I could see was your face. You were smiling at the kids and parents. I could tell you weren't faking it; you truly wanted to teach those kids."

That memory still makes me feel good.

"Then a parent moved, and I saw your delicious curves wonderfully displayed in that red wraparound dress of yours. I was glad I was wearing a long shirt and there were so many other parents to greet you. By the time it was my turn to talk to you, I had my body under control."

"I did not know."

"Some days, after seeing you, I'd shut myself in my room and jerk off thinking of you."

"Me too."

"What?" Did I understand correctly?

"Not after seeing you. I was usually at school then. When I went home, in the shower or in bed, I'd think of you when I touched myself."

She stares at me, a red tint on her cheeks.

The knot of anxiety in my gut eases.

"What else did you do while you thought of me?"

"Sometimes I used BOB."

"Bob?" The shot of jealousy I feel is so strong, I can't help the growl in my voice.

She glances at the window.

"Battery operated boyfriend, my vibrator."

Laughter bubbles through me.

She wraps the blanket tightly around her.

I kiss her. Pick her up and place her on my lap. Her back is stiff.

"I was laughing with relief, not at you, baby."

"I've never said I love you to a woman, but when I was making love to you and saw your eyes, I knew you were the woman I want to spend the rest of my life with."

Layla relaxes, brushes a stray lock away from my face.

I wait, hoping she feels the same way.

"Do you mean it?"

There's a vulnerability in the way she says the words.

"I love your kindness, the way you give everything to your kids–I'm like that with my patients too. Talking with you is fun. And I love the way you aided me and my family help Evie learn to trust again."

A tear runs down one of her cheeks.

"Hey, it's okay if you don't feel the same way. I won't pressure you. Just give me a few dates before you decide."

"I love you, Fallon. I thought you'd never be interested in someone like me."

I'm grinning like a cheshire cat, but I don't care. I kiss her reverently.

Layla laughs too.

Then I remember her last words. "What do you mean, someone like you?"

She shrugs.

I hold her shoulders. "Look baby, I've never had a proper relationship before. So, please be honest with me, cause I don't know what I'm doing."

"Well, you're more experienced and older than me. I thought you might like the more sophisticated woman."

"All my sexual partners were sophisticated. I never wanted to marry them, like I do with you."

She searches my face. "Is this a marriage proposal?"

My heart thuds against my chest. I feel like everything that happened in my life was leading me to this moment.

"Yes."

She looks away from me. That's what she does when something is worrying or upsetting her.

"Tell me. Honesty, remember?"

"I was engaged before I moved to Blossom Ford. I found out my fiancée was cheating on me with my best friend."

"Oh, Baby. They didn't deserve you. That excuse of a man is an asshole!"

"I agree. But one reason why he was having doubts about marrying me was my body. Apparently, women with a huge ass like mine are great for fucking but not marriage. I wouldn't fit with his worker friends' nicely proportioned girlfriends."

"He wasn't man enough for you."

Outside, the wind howls.

"Hear that? Even nature agrees with me. I love your breasts and tiny waist just as much as I love your bounties ass and hips–they are part of what makes you Layla. I believe God made you for me. Because I love every fucking thing about you, girl."

CHAPTER EIGHT

Fallon

I PARK THE truck outside my house after dropping off Layla and climb out. It's Sunday morning, and the sky is bright blue. The only signs of yesterday's freak storm are the deep snow and the handful of branches that littered some roads as Layla and I drove into town.

I climb the porch steps, then freeze when the door flies open. Evie sprints outside and flings herself into my arms. I catch her, narrowly avoiding falling down the steps.

She locks her short arms around my neck and breaks into sobs.

"What's the matter, sweetheart?" Alarm spreads through me.

Gently, I try to pry her away from me so I can see her. She won't budge.

"What happened?" I ask Mom when she appears at the door, her apron covered in flour.

"She's just worried about you," Mom answers.

I watch her disappear inside, then sit on the porch swing with Evie on my lap. I pat her back.

"I'm fine sweetheart," I say.

More sobs.

It breaks my heart to see her so upset. I should have guessed this might happen. Since the day we met, last night was the first we didn't sleep in the same house. Evie's mom was already hospitalized by the time she introduced us. Evie was living with a caregiver. I asked for leave, moved to Maryland and spent the two months before her mom passed living with her.

Even when I took Evie to live with me in New York and returned to work, I made sure I was home to tuck her into bed.

"You said you'd never leave," Evie says in between sniffles, still clinging to me like a monkey.

I think about how to answer.

"What did Granny say?"

I called Mom earlier in the morning once the phone lines started working again. As I'd guessed, she'd figured out I'd found shelter. Although we don't get many storms in Blossom Ford, most of the locals are always prepared for such eventualities.

"You were sheltering from the storm."

"That's right. That means Daddy will come home when the storm passes, right?"

No answer.

"Something like that might happen again, or if someone is very ill, I might have to help them get better. I'll always come home, though."

I carry on patting Evie's shoulder. Her mom loved her and fought to stay with her, but she still left. My little girl knows that sometimes, wanting to stay is not enough.

"Would you like to go to Jackson's Diner to have a strawberry sundae?" It's her favorite dessert.

She lifts her head. Finally, looks at me.

"With extra strawberry sauce?"

This isn't the time to worry about her teeth.

"You can have triple extra sauce."

"Silly Daddy! That'd be too sweet!"

I chuckle.

"Come on, you'll get a cold if we stay here any longer."

She holds onto my hand as we enter the house.

Layla and I agreed to talk to Evie together on Wednesday, after school. It's early release day, so we'll have plenty of time to chat. I tamp down the worry over how Evie might react. Right now, she must be my priority. If that means Layla and I have to wait before we can be together, we'll bear it.

***

Layla

I REACH THE place Fallon and I agreed is best to chat with Evie. It's a family restaurant with a play area, a half hour drive outside of Blossom Ford. Fallon suggested we come together, but I didn't want to take the chance of rumors spreading before we told Evie about our relationship. That's also why we can only talk to each other on the phone for now. Well, that and the fact I haven't talked to the school principal about dating a parent.

I get a corner table and ask for chamomile tea. I need to calm the butterflies flying around in my stomach. Just because Evie loves me as a teacher doesn't mean she'll be happy to see me marry her dad.

I wave to Fallon and Evie when they come through the door. Even though we saw each other a couple of hours ago, Evie hugs me. While the waitress takes our order, she chats about the nativity play.

"Miss. Shah said I'm bright because I know all my lines, even though we have two days to perform," Evie tells her dad.

Fallon pats her head and compliments her.

Evie glances at him, then at me.

"Poppet, remember how I said Miss. Shah and I want to talk to you?"

Evie bobs her head.

Fallon takes her hand.

"Miss. Shah and I like each other a lot. If it's okay

with you, we want to get married."

My heart is in my mouth.

Evie looks at me.

"That's true, Sweetheart. We won't do anything if you're not okay with it." I hold her other hand, meaning every word. If my happiness means hurting her, I don't want it.

Evie shoves her chair back and runs out.

Fallon heads after her. I follow him out.

Evie is sitting on one swing in the play area. She's facing away from us, but I saw her look back, probably to check her dad was following. I hold Fallon's arm.

"Can you let me talk to her first?"

There's anguish in his grey eyes.

"I'll wait here."

Deliberately, I move slowly to give Evie more thinking time. I sit on the adjacent swing, waiting.

"Will mom still be my mom? Can I carry on talking about her?"

My heart breaks a little. I want to hug her. I hold myself back.

"She'll always be your mom, sweetheart, even if one day you feel like calling me mom too. The memories you have with her keep her alive in your heart. And she was a very special person, because she made you."

She stares at the ground. Then glances at Fallon.

"Are you worried I might steal your dad?"

She giggles.

"Your dad is a little worried I might steal you away

from him because I love you so much and he feels I'm better at talking to you and making you laugh."

"Sometimes, Daddy is a little silly. I love being with you, but he's my dad."

"And you love him?"

She nods.

"Do you remember what Ricky wrote in the worry box in the classroom a while back?"

"He was worried about having a new dad. Last week he shared his new dad plays soccer with him every Sunday. He said he likes it because his mom was terrible at playing soccer."

I smile.

"He got to name his baby sister, too. He listens to his mom's tummy with his dad and talks to the baby. I think now he loves his new dad."

"They became a new family, just like we could be."

Evie nods. It's a start. She's willing to try to become a family. It'll be up to me and Fallon to make sure we make a happy and safe home for her.

CHAPTER NINE

Fallon

I'M OUTSIDE LAYLA'S apartment on Friday night, waiting for her to answer the door. It's ten o'clock and I'm wondering if she's already gone to bed when the door opens.

"What are you doing here?"

She drags me inside, then checks the corridor before closing the door.

"I couldn't wait to see you. Now that you've spoken with your principal, we don't need to hide our relationship."

She's wearing a bathrobe that hugs her curves. Damp tendrils of hair peek out of the towel wrapped around her head. My already hard cock pulses.

"What about Evie?"

"She fell asleep around eight. The excitement of the

nativity play and Christmas class party exhausted her. She won't wake up."

My eyes lock on the bare skin of her collarbone.

"My parents are watching T.V. I sneaked out. I'll go back at the crack of dawn, before Evie wakes up. Or, if you're tired, I'll leave. You had a long day."

I wish I didn't sound so needy. It's just after making love with Layla last Saturday, I want her more than before. My dick doesn't seem to understand the issues we had to sort out before we could get together.

"I was restless." She lifts her arms and removes the towel from her head. Her breasts rise. Helplessly, I track the sensual glide, my body a willing slave to her charms.

She lets the towel drop and fluffs her hair, watching me.

I shrug out of my coat, not caring where it falls. She pulls me close, her hands sliding to my belt.

"Baby." I kiss her, the taste of her mouth and the movement of her hands as she unzips me, driving me wild.

I turn and bend her over the wooden chest in the corridor. She spreads her legs and turns over her shoulder, the need in her hazel eyes almost tangible.

"Hurry."

As I struggle to get my dick out of my pants, Layla lifts her robe, exposing her caramel ass and her dripping pussy.

"You're ready for me," my voice is thick with desire.

I guide myself to her entrance and hold her hip with my free hand. I ram into her, hissing at the pleasure of her muscles gripping me.

Layla arches her back and pushes against me, matching my every thrust.

I squeeze her large buttocks, massaging the smooth, round globes. "I really love your ass, baby. Watching your back stretched out like this makes me feel like a king."

"So good, Fallon, don't stop."

I don't know if I can stop. My cock is on fire, each time I drive into Layla bringing me closer to orgasm.

I reach around her front and lift her closer. I fondle her breasts, roll the nipples.

She moans and snakes an arm round the back of my neck.

I glide a hand over her pussy and rub her clit. Her moans grow louder, driving me ever closer to the edge, making it impossible to hold on. When I bite the side of her neck, she shatters, the pull of her muscles forcing me to an orgasm so strong, my whole-body shudders.

When my heart stops pounding, I lift a sleepy Layla into my arms, but remember just in time that my trousers are hanging down my legs. I grin stupidly at myself.

"Layla, point to the bedroom."

I could have searched for it if my legs were clear, but not in this state.

"Right door." She blinks, trying to keep her eyes

open.

It takes a while to shuffle through her living room. The door is open, so I pass through and put Layla on the bed. Finally, I step away from my trousers and get us both under the covers.

"I can't believe I fell asleep." Layla burrows into my chest, as graceful as a cat.

"You had a crazy week."

I rub her back, frowning.

Something doesn't feel right. Then I remember.

"Layla."

"Hmm?"

"Are you sleeping?"

I lift her face towards me, so I can see her.

"No, but I will be soon. What is it?"

"I love you."

She smiles.

"I love you too."

"That's why I couldn't wait until our date tomorrow. I had to tell you that. It felt wrong to say it over the phone, since it's the first time. But when I realized you were naked under your robe, all I could think about was getting inside you."

"That was nice."

"Are you really okay, about school, I mean?"

"The principal wasn't exactly pleased. He said since Blossom Ford is small, there have been other couples like us. While Evie is in my class, the school will monitor me to make sure I'm not showing favoritism to Evie, just so they have a way to counter any complaints from parents. There might be some gossip about us. It's worth it, though, to have you and Evie for the rest of my life."

"The gossip will die down when folks see how happy we are. The monitoring is going to be hard on you, though."

"I'm a teacher. I had several observations whilst training."

"It's not the same thing, though."

"It's temporary. And we're lucky; some schools don't allow it all. Besides, Mom was my teacher in fourth grade. I had to call her Mrs. Shah at school and didn't get away with anything. I told the principal that, I think it helped him feel I can handle the situation. "

Maybe it's just as well I'm starting work at the hospital in the New Year, so Dad will take Evie to School. It might be easier for other parents if they don't see me often.

A soft snore makes me realize Layla's asleep. I listen to her gentle snores, happy that I'm learning something new about her. I can't wait to learn more.

Layla turned me into someone who wants to grow old with a woman. Since I was ten, when I helplessly saw my little sister lose her life after a car accident, I was determined to be an emergency doctor, so I'd have the knowledge to help save lives in a similar situation. Saving lives, treating patients became my passion.

I love my job so much, I thought it was all I needed

to be happy. Even after Evie entered my life, I thought work and my daughter would be more than enough.

Layla changed that. With only a week to go till Christmas day, she is the best Christmas gift I've ever received in my life.

EPILOGUE

Layla

Five Years Later

THE SOUND OF our three-year-old daughter Katie chuckling through the baby monitor wakes me up.

"It's okay. We don't need to get up yet. Let's rest longer, please." Fallon tightens his arms around me.

"Is Evie with her?"

Katie worships her big sister. She follows her everywhere, her chubby legs struggling to keep up with the twelve-year-old girl, who's growing so fast, she might be as tall as her six-feet-three dad.

"For now, she loves her sister's attention, but soon, when Katie's six or seven and Evie is fifteen or sixteen, she won't. It'll be just like me and Verlin."

I laugh, but talking about Fallon's brother reminds me that staying in bed while we can is a great idea. I used to think Christmas at my parents was a huge event. It's painless compared to holidays at the

O'Connors, which is an enjoyable, yet exhausting affair.

Fallon's eight brothers and their wives, as well as many grandkids, cram into one house and consume a humongous amount of food.

It helps that Fallon built our house yards away from his parents' and siblings' homes. After stuffing ourselves with turkey, we only have to walk a few steps.

I love we take turns spending the holidays here and at my parents in Garnet City.

"Which dress do you want to wear?" Evie asks.

There's a gurgling sound, then Katie answers. "Pink."

"Pink what?"

"Pink, please."

Fallon kisses my nose. "Evie sounds just like you."

When we visit Garnet City, even people who don't know us say that.

The sound of children chattering reaches us from the window.

"Mom, Dad, we're going to Grannie's. Uncle Rio is here," Evie shouts.

We hear footsteps on the stairs, then the bang of the front door. The noise outside grows louder. Riordan is Fallon's second eldest brother, if I count Patrick, who's Auntie Caitlin's only son, as the eldest brother.

"I can't believe how gentle Riordan is with the kids, for an ex-military man. They all behave so well with him," I say.

"He treats them like little soldiers. He even gave them ranks." Fallon shakes his head, the smile playing around his mouth showing how proud he is of the brother the family nearly lost.

"Are you a little jealous?" I tease.

Fallon can easily handle our girls, but when all the O'Connor grandkids are together, he sweats.

"Mrs. O'Connor, there are so many things I can do well. Shall I show them to you?"

I yelp as Fallon flips me on my back. He traces my lips then inserts a finger into my mouth and my laughter turns into heated need.

The End

MARRYING THE PROTECTIVE PROFESSOR

CURVY BRIDES OF BLOSSOM FORD #1

August

ALL MY LIFE I've secretly wished I was born and raised in an ordinary family, with loving, welcoming parents instead of being the town's sign of bad luck, growing up at Blossom Ford Orphanage and having the town's name as my surname, like the other kids there. I can't help believing if I was wanted, the acceptance and sense of belonging would have helped me become someone who knows how to love. That belief is strongest when I think of Ella Mitchell.

It's Friday night so ensuring she gets home safely is my top priority as I park my SUV a short distance from Jackson's Diner where she's working, far enough to see the door of the restaurant but not so close that anyone might link my presence to the diner. I don't care how the interfering residents of Blossom Ford view me, but I don't want rumors to spread about Ella.

I slide down the car seat, getting comfortable even as I curse myself for the warmth that spreads through my chest at the mere thought of her name. As I've done a millionth time, I tell myself I'm here to protect her.

An uncomfortable tightness in my chest and a bitter taste in my mouth that I'm all too familiar with have me exhaling slowly. But it's hard to chase away the guilt. I cannot keep from committing the same sin. I'm a scarred, divorced, grizzly mountain of a man that's old enough to be her father while she's a beautiful, innocent twenty-two-year-old with her whole life ahead of her. Ella deserves better than me. But I still can't stop thinking about her.

It makes no difference that what I feel for her is more than physical attraction. I love her strength, soft smile and the way she's warm to everyone that crosses paths with her. There's a certainty in my bones that she's meant for me alone. This only makes the guilt worse. I should let her go because I love her.

And I have. To a point. For the last two years since I returned to Blossom Ford, saw her for the first time and fell for the kindness in her honey hued eyes and the sweetest curves I'd ever seen, I've stopped myself from approaching her. From claiming her. At least in real life. Because in my dreams, I've made love to her every single night and spent my days laughing with her. I've always considered my self-control one of my strongest attributes, but I can't stop dreaming about her.

I can't help the fact that I won't have her driving home by herself at midnight, after her shifts at the diner on Fridays and Saturdays. If I'm an asshole, so be it. And if deep down I know as well as ensuring she's safe, I have to see her face, I'll take the guilt and deal with it.

I frown when only two cars remain in the parking lot. One is old Jackson's beat up truck, and the other belongs to Rosie; the woman who works with Ella. Ella's old yellow mini should be right besides Rosie's.

The door to the diner flies open and Rosie marches out in her apron, phone glued to her ear. She sprints to her car. My frown thickens. How is Ella going to get home? Will she be closing on her own? I force myself to stay in the car. As much as I want to rush in and help, keeping a distance is crucial to my self-discipline.

I ramp up the air conditioning in the car a little higher. It usually takes one hour to close, but tonight, it'll take Ella longer. Old Jackson doesn't think hard work hurts women. There's no way he's going to help with setting the dinner to the way he likes it.

I keep my eyes on the door and an hour and a half later, I'm rewarded with the sight of Ella's curvy hips wrapped in hugging denim and the soft way her breasts hug her blouse. Even after a ten-hour shift, she's a vision that gets my heart racing.

She zeroes in on my car and it's like she can see me, like she knows I'm waiting here for her. She does this on Fridays and Saturdays; the days I wait for her. If she worked any other nights, I'd wait for her then, too. She's friends with Mrs. Gallagher, the orphanage director who's the closest thing to a mother I've ever had. Ella must think of me as a much older brother who's looking out for her.

She steps on the street and heads towards me. I know that she's just taking the road to her house, but I can't stop my heart from beating even faster. It's like this every time I see her.

I'm feeling something else too; anger. Her walking alone down the empty street at this time of the night is pissing me off.

She's only a few feet from me when a car careens down the street and stops beside her. I sit up straight, hoping a friend is coming to pick her up. But she doesn't slow down, even after spotting the car.

I scowl as a man stumbles out of the car and steps in her path. It's Toby Anderson, Ella's ex. Something ugly rears in me. Despite my unstoppable feelings for Ella, whenever I see him, I realize how great my self-control is. Every time I saw him with Ella, I wanted to knock him out. The four months they dated were an exercise in self-discipline I didn't think I was going to win. But for Ella, to give her the chance at happiness she deserved with someone her age that could give her a comfortable life, I held myself back.

I don't like the way Toby sways on his feet. The light from the full moon and lamppost in front of the diner are enough to make out the disgust on Ella's face.

Before I know it, my hand is on the door handle, but my eyes don't stray from Toby.

They are talking but the loud music and shouts from the car stop me from hearing what they are saying. Toby reaches out a hand and touches Ella's arm. She wrenches it back.

I'm out of the car. I sprint towards them, her safety the only thought in my mind. for her, I'd tried staying away, but her safety is something I'll not compromise on. even if it means she might hate me for interfering with her life.

FAKE MARRYING THE BODYGUARD

THE O'CONNORS OF BLOSSOM FORD #4

Bonnie

I KEEP MY eyes tightly shut and listen for noises around me. It's too quiet. I'm used to the sounds of cars honking, people going about the apartment. Then a sudden high sound startles me and I grab the bed sheet. I take a while to work out it's a bird call.

When my heart settles, I can tell I'm alone. I know the feeling of being watched all too well; this isn't it. I allow myself to open my eyes and stare around an unfamiliar, semi dark room. Instead of white stone walls and marble floors, there are wooden walls and floors.

My breath hitches when I notice the large window opposite me. The sun is setting and the deep orange and pink colors inside the golden ball are breathtaking. There are trees outside with some of their leaves turning a burnt orange; it's a mesmerizing depiction of fall. A little while later, I realize I'm still staring and pull myself up on it.

I don't know where I am, so why am I admiring the view? I'm usually so vigilant about my environment. Have I finally gone mad, like Dad always said I would one day?

I shake my head. I move the soft bed sheet aside and look down at my body, taking in the white dress.

Memories of Rory, the wedding and escaping the life I lived for twenty years return.

I must have fallen asleep on the way here. This must be his cabin.

A soft knock sounds. My eyes shift to the door. Heart pounding, I tumble out of the massive bed and stand. I try to answer, but no sound comes out of my mouth. I clear my throat and try again, using all my acting skills to strengthen my voice.

"Yes?" There's no sign of the nerves trying to strangle my throat. I hide my trembling hands behind my back.

"It's Rory. Can I open the door?"

Even if he hadn't identified himself, I would have known it was him. There was something unique about the lilting rhythm of his deep voice. It made me want to relax around him, want to trust him.

When I say yes, he opens the door but doesn't leg to of it. Light enters the room, allowing me to see the way his sea-green eyes rove over me before they return to my face. Some of the tension leaves me. His gaze is familiar, he's looked at me like that countless times in the year he's guarded me.

What's different is his attire. I've never seen him in anything other than a white shirt and dark suit. He's wearing a t-shirt that outlines his muscles and low hanging blue jeans. My heart skips a beat and this time it has nothing to do with nerves. His auburn hair is wet, as if he's just come out of a shower. He looks younger than his forty-one years. More approachable. I swallow, struggling with my unsuitable and unwanted attraction to this man, who just happens to be my husband.

"Dinner is ready. Come have a bite, lass."

Why does it feel like he's showering me with affection whenever he calls me by that word? I can feel my nose crinkle as I try to stare him down, to figure out why he used that word. He stares back blankly, then shuts the door, leaving me in semidarkness again.

I bring my hands in front of me. Even though my heart is still racing and my body feels alive, my fingers are steady. I'm attracted to but not scared of him.

Can I really trust Rory the way my body seems to believe it can? Or have I escaped from my controlling father only to fall into the hands of a more wicked monster?

I didn't always feel like I could trust Rory. Dad contracted his personal bodyguard services firm after the company he previously used failed to catch my stalker for three years. The stalker had become more dangerous, nearly kidnapped me once.

That's when Dad brought Rory in, even though he seemed to have reservations about hiring the ex-Mixed Martial Arts athlete. I'd never understood that. The Red King, as Rory was called by those in the sport, was Dad's favorite fighter. Now, maybe I do. He seems decent, somehow different from Dad.

The men that guarded me were also my jailors. I'd learned the hard way that all the workers in the house, no matter their position, were Dad's people. Rory terrified me the most. First, for the same reason Dad loved the MMA fighter. His explosive, merciless fighting style. It made me think he was cruel. The other reason was scarier. For the first time in seven years, I was behaving like a high school girl with a severe crush. I did my damnedest to hide my growing attraction.

But only three months later, his security team caught the stalker when he attempted to kidnap me again. Rory's powerful arms had held me against the strong column of his chest and stroked my damp hair.

"You're safe, lass," he'd said softly, emotion lacing his voice as if he really cared about me.

I told myself he was doing his job, that he was the type of competitive person who had to always win and the emotion in that ragged, comforting voice of his was pride. However, since then, it became almost impossible to hide my attraction. Worse, I'm developing feelings for him.

The way he interacted with me didn't change but I

began putting a different meaning to his cryptic once overs when he started a shift. I couldn't shake the feeling he was checking to see if I was alright.

After watching him for six months since the stalking incident, I worked up the courage to ask him for help. I had to escape from Dad. My life had become a survival game long ago, and I was exhausted from living that way. I sang and smiled for crowds, but I'd lost my passion for singing, the only thing that gave me joy for so long.

To the public, I was a bubbly singer with millions of fans, but my private life comprised long hours of practice, rigorous diets and exercises imposed by Dad. I had tried escaping once, only to be brought back by one of my so-called bodyguards. He controlled my fortune and made decisions about my welfare. My will to live was disappearing at the thought of having to live that way for the rest of my life.

One day, while I was out doing the exercises Dad insisted on, I pretended to fall. When Rory helped me up, I explained how Dad was blackmailing me with two videos he took of me thrashing his study when I was seventeen and twenty-one. He was threatening to have me put under a conservatorship. I have no memory of vandalizing his study, but it was me in those videos. I suspected Dad drugged me, but had no way of proving that.

I was ready to give him all my fortune if he could help me flee. If he will enter a temporary marriage contract with me, before Dad got wind of anything, it'd be extremely hard to impose a conservatorship when I had a spouse willing to testify my mental capacity was sound. Especially if it was someone as influential as Rory.

"What if I do the same thing your dad is doing? I could keep your money and control you the way he does," Rory had asked, sea-green eyes steady on mine, as he crouched beside me on the green grass of the park.

It was the start of summer and a hot day but I went ice cold. I'd searched his face, lack of trust in my ability to judge people strong. Since the age of five, I grew up with Dad telling me people couldn't be trusted, that they didn't care for me. The only thing they loved was my voice and the smiling singer Bonnie. Maybe I was wrong about Rory.

I'd strengthened my back, focused on his steady gaze.

"I won't carry on the way I am."

"Okay, lass. I'll draft the papers. The only way to make sure you're permanently safe is to get those files, anything else he might have, and find something on him to make him believe if he ever tries to control you again, he'll be ruined."

"Is that possible?" My heart was in my mouth.

"Nothing is impossible where humans are concerned."

It took Rory three months to get everything sorted. Three long months of hope and fear. Usually, Dad left me alone, trusting in the army of people he'd placed around me to report my daily life. We had lunch together once a month at his favorite restaurant. I thought he'd see something was up, that I'd mustered the courage to flee. When he suspected nothing, I was so thankful he'd forced me to take acting classes.

Rory and his team found out Dad was involved with an organized crime ring of underage prostitution. A friend of his married us before Rory threatened Dad with providing proof of his illegal activities to the police if he ever tried to force me back to him.

I switch on the bedside lamp and gaze around the room. My one suitcase and guitar are under the window. I remove a flowing maxi dress and run my fingers through the soft fabric. It's one of the few dresses I'd hidden from Dad.

No matter how much he controlled my diet and exercises, my chubbiness never went away. His solution, which never really worked, was to have me wear body-shaping outfits at home, too. For a while now, I have hoped to wear maxi dresses whenever I wanted.

I get clean underwear and toiletries. I'm a little fazed that there's no ensuite in the bedroom, but I shake it off. Compared to the fact I might live life my way, it's only a minute drawback.

Rory's standing by the sink when I open the door. I was quiet but he must have heard, because he turns around. He's wearing a white apron knitted with a large picture of one of the Sesame Street characters. It covers almost all the apron.

A chuckle comes out of me before I can stop myself.

"Something funny?" His face is impassive.

It only causes me to crack up again. I cover my mouth with my free hand, unsure of what to say. My eyes refuse to move away from the knitted character. It looks so alive.

"My Mom and Aunt Caitlin made this apron especially for me. It's one of my favorites."

"It's beautiful. I mean, it looks good on you."

His lips lift.

My hands tighten on my clothes. Because I've just gone from humor to heat in a heartbeat. My cheeks flush. I can't drag my eyes away from that sexy face of his. I've never seen Rory smile like this. Like he doesn't have a care in the world, like an innocent boy.

"Do you mean it?" He asks.

"Mean what?"

"This overall looks good on me."

Did his eyes darken? He's no longer smiling, but I'm not exactly worried. Something about the way he's watching me is putting my body on alert. A panty melting kind of alert.

"Where's the bathroom?" I ask, unsure of what the tension between us means.

He points to a closed door and I dash in, locking the door. I wash and dress slowly, going over our conversation again and again, but I can't work out the meaning behind the expression in his eyes.

I give myself a stern lecture before I exit the bathroom. I've just left one prison. My body may feel Rory is safe, but I don't know him well.

Right now, Dad is petrified of what Rory might do, so sticking to him gives me the best protection against being dragged back to my old life. However, still I have to be careful of Rory and any people I meet.

Even if Rory has no evil intentions towards me, I still must keep myself from falling further for him. No matter how much I wish he were truly in love with me and wanted to spend the rest of his life with me, it's not likely to happen. What could a successful, ruggedly handsome man in his prime like Rory, want with an insecure, inexperienced, chubby woman like me, when he has the world's most beautiful women vying for his attention?

OTHER BOOKS BY THE AUTHOR

CURVY BRIDES OF BLOSSOM FORD SERIES

MARRYING THE PROTECTIVE PROFESSOR

MARRYING THE GRUMPY DIRECTOR

MARRYING THE POSSESSIVE NEIGHBOR

MARRYING THE WIDOWED DOCTOR

MARRYING THE SCARRED SOLDIER

MARRYING THE OBSESSIVE CEO

MARRYING THE BIG MOUNTAIN MAN

THE O'CONNORS OF BLOSSOM FORD SERIES

MATCHED TO PATRICK

REDEEMING THE MOUNTAIN MAN

BROTHER'S BEST FRIEND OBSESSION

FAKE MARRYING THE BODYGUARD

ABOUT THE AUTHOR

Iris West writes short and spicy romance about alpha heroes and the women they can't help falling in love with. She loves reading all types of romance books that have a happy ending and is an avid Kdrama fan.

You can follow or like her on **Facebook, Instagram** Tik Tok and/or **Goodreads.**

FREE BOOK

Would you like a free book? Sign up to my mailing list at https://dl.bookfunnel.com/t191w45ryj to receive a copy of Loving My Fake Husband, a Curvy Brides of Blossom Ford short story.

HELP OTHERS FIND THIS BOOK

Thank you for reading Single Dad's Christmas Gift. If you enjoyed this book, please help others discover it by leaving a review at your favorite online bookstore.

Many thanks,

Iris xx